JAMES

PERCY

THERE ARE 36 EXCITING THOMAS TITLES TO COLLECT IN THE BUZZ BOOK SERIES

Look out for all our other books
about Thomas and his friends
available from Heinemann,
Mammoth and Dean

First published in Great Britain 1991 by Buzz Books
an imprint of Reed Children's Books
Michelin House, 81 Fulham Road, London SW3 6RB
and Auckland, Melbourne, Singapore and Toronto
Reprinted 1993 (twice) and 1994 (twice)

Adapted from the television story by
Britt Allcroft and David Mitton

ISBN 1 85591 117 5

Printed in Italy by Olivotto

THOMAS AND TREVOR

buzz books

Trevor the Traction Engine enjoys living in the vicarage orchard on the Island of Sodor. Edward the Blue Engine once helped to save him from being turned into scrap so now Trevor lives at the vicarage and the two engines are great friends.

Edward comes to see Trevor every day.
Sometimes Trevor is sad because he doesn't
have enough work to do.

8

"I do like to keep busy all the time,"
Trevor sighed one day, "and I do like
company, especially children's company."

"Cheer up," smiled Edward. "The Fat Controller has work for you at his new harbour – I'm to take you to meet Thomas today."

"Oh!" exclaimed Trevor happily. "A harbour, the seaside, children, that will be lovely."

'Trevor's truck was coupled behind Edward and they set off to meet Thomas.

Thomas was on his way to the harbour with a trainload of metal pilings. They were needed to make the harbour wall firm and safe.

"Hello, Thomas," said Edward. "This is Trevor, a friend of mine. He's a Traction Engine."

Thomas eyed the newcomer doubtfully. "A *what* engine?" he asked.

"A Traction Engine," explained Trevor. "I run on roads instead of rails. Can you take me to the harbour, please? The Fat Controller has a job for me."

"Yes – of course," replied Thomas. But he was still puzzled.

Workmen coupled Trevor's truck to Thomas's train and soon they were ready to start their journey.

"I'm glad the Fat Controller needs me,"

called Trevor. "I don't have enough to do sometimes, you know, although I can work anywhere – in orchards, on farms, in scrapyards, even at harbours."

"But you don't run on rails," puffed
Thomas.

"I'm a Traction Engine – I don't need rails
to be useful," replied Trevor. "You wait and
see."

When they reached the harbour they found everything in confusion. Trucks had been derailed, blocking the line, and stone slabs lay everywhere.

"We must get these pilings through," said
Thomas's driver. "They are essential.
Trevor," he said, "we need you to drag
them round this mess."

"Just the sort of job I like," replied Trevor. "Now you'll see, Thomas – I'll soon show you what Traction Engines can do."

Trevor was as good as his word. First he dragged the stones clear with chains. Then he towed the pilings into position.

"Who needs rails?" he muttered cheerfully to himself.

Later Thomas brought his two coaches, Annie and Clarabel, to visit Trevor.

Thomas was most impressed. "Now I understand how useful a traction engine can be," he said.

Thomas's coaches were full of children
and Trevor gave them rides along the
harbour. Of all the jobs he did at the
harbour that day, he liked this best of all.

"He's very kind," said Annie.

"He reminds me of Thomas," added Clarabel.

24

Everyone was sorry when it was time for
Trevor to go. Thomas pulled him to the
junction.

A small tear came into Trevor's eye. Thomas pretended not to see and whistled gaily to make Trevor happy.

"I'll come and see you if I can," Thomas promised. "The Vicar will look after you,

and there's plenty of work for you now at the orchard, but we may need you again at the harbour some day."

"That would be wonderful," said Trevor happily.

That evening, Trevor stood in the orchard remembering his new friend, Thomas, the harbour and most of all – the children. Then he went happily to sleep in the shed at the bottom of the orchard.

THOMAS

EDWAR

GORDON